Quentin Blake

MR FILKINS IN THE DESERT

TATE

The sun shone down on Mr Filkins as he walked through the desert.

He was on his way to celebrate his 90th birthday with his granddaughter Miranda and her family.

He had eaten all his cream cheese sandwiches but fortunately he still had some sparkling mineral water in a bottle in his backpack.

It was a very hot day and a very long journey.

Sometimes he wondered if he would ever get there.

He knew that the desert
was full of unpleasant
creatures.

Once he had to hide
behind a rock to avoid
a two-headed Snerg.

Later on he climbed a
tree as a forty-legged
Clutterbunk went past.

He was thinking how lucky he was not to have encountered the most unpleasant creature of all when suddenly in front of him there it was – the fearsome Zagobert!

But what a state it was in!

It was lying on the ground, its seven legs stretched out beside it.

Its tail had gone limp, three of its eyes were closed, and it was gasping painfully.

'Oh dear,' Mr Filkins said to himself, 'it obviously needs something to drink.'

He got out his bottle
of sparkling mineral
water and looked at it.

'Just enough for two.'

The effect was amazing.

The Zagobert stood up on
all of its seven legs, its tail
was waving and its eyes
were looking in all directions.

One of them must
have seen Mr Filkins,
because a leg stretched
out and lifted him onto
the Zagobert's back,
and off they went!

Over huge
craggy rocks –

Over hundreds of cactuses –

Over a forest
of dead trees –

And then, suddenly,
they were at Miranda's.

All the family were
there to greet Mr Filkins –
Gizmo, Fred, Samantha,
Oswald and Emily-Francesca.

What a birthday party it was!

There was a cake with nine candles,
    Swiss rolls and chocolate eclairs,
        strawberries, raspberries, pears and bananas,
        kiwi delight –

            and lots and lots of
                sparkling mineral water.

Everyone enjoyed it.

And so did the Zagobert!

For Dick Edwards
and the Hastings
Storytelling Festival

First published 2021 by order of the Tate Trustees
by Tate Publishing, a division of Tate Enterprises Ltd,
Millbank, London SW1P 4RG

www.tate.org.uk/publishing

Text and illustrations © Quentin Blake 2021

A catalogue record for this book is available from the British Library

ISBN 978 1 84976 750 7

Distributed in the United States and Canada by ABRAMS, New York
Library of Congress Control Number applied for

Colour reproduction by DL Imaging Ltd, London
Printed in China by Toppan Leefung Printing Ltd